ANNA and the BABY BUZZARD

by Helga Sandburg
illustrated by Brinton Turkle

BUZZARD

When Anna found the baby buzzard scrunched up in the cave and brought it home, everyone said, "Nobody anywhere ever likes a buzzard."

But Anna was stubborn. She kept the baby buzzard and cleaned it and fed it and trained it, and when it grew into a beautiful black bird with a six-foot wingspread, she knew she had named it right: *Glory*!

Anna's story is based on the scientific concept of "imprinting," according to which a creature of one species may learn to see itself as the child of another. It is the story of a warm, funny, and unusual relationship between Anna and Glory, and of Anna's own growth through it.

The plentiful two-color illustrations gracefully capture the sunny moods of summer and friendship.

ANNA and the BABY BUZZARD

by Helga Sandburg
illustrated by Brinton Turkle

E. P. DUTTON & CO., INC. NEW YORK

First Edition

Published simultaneously in Canada by Clarke, Irwin & Company
Limited, Toronto and Vancouver
SBN: 0-525-25769-1 (Trade)   SBN: 0-525-25770-5 (DLLB)
Library of Congress Catalog Card Number: 76-81712

jS2135an

For Lenore

To the Reader

There was a real baby buzzard and its name was Lenore. I loved it and this book was written because of my adventure with Lenore.

Whenever a young bird or animal is separated from its mother at birth or before it can take care of itself, it regards whoever cares for it as its parent. This is called "imprinting," and it causes the most unlikely creatures to get along well with each other.

I found a baby turkey vulture one spring in a pine stump and called it Lenore and raised it. When it flew away in fall, it was as beautiful as the buzzard in this make-believe story. Lenore came back for a visit the next spring and then went away again. If you see a buzzard soaring someday, you may be looking at my Lenore. Say hello for me.

Helga Sandburg
Cleveland, Ohio

There were two of them in the cave in the woods. They were a month old and downy and white and the size of barnyard hens, like those that lived at the farm in the valley below the hill. The light was dusky in the cave, and it was comfortable, and their mother brought them food.

They heard the beating of her great black wings as she flew down through the trees with a piece of food in her beak for their lunch that she had found somewhere. She landed on the ground outside and walked in and dropped it before them and went away again. They hissed, excited, and dragged the food back into the cave. They held it with their big four-toed feet and pulled it apart and ate it, greedy.

All they saw of the world where their mother went searching for food every day was stony, mossy, uneven ground, and always just before dark, under the roof of their cave, a red ball of fire falling slowly through trunks of trees. Sometimes it rained or the warm June wind blew by, scented of daisies and clover and cows and sheep and sunny pastures, but the baby birds knew nothing of these. They heard wood

thrushes and sparrows singing somewhere, and in a nest in a nearby tree, young crows that they never saw were continually talking together. Sometimes a cow bawled far away, or a sheep called or a human shouted, but they didn't know what the sounds were.

One sunset they caught sight of a girl with yellow pigtails and bare feet running down through the woods and a little boy after her, calling:

"Anna! Wait for me!"

This afternoon the same boy was shouting the same

words as he came up the hill on the heels of the same girl. The birds watched the bare legs dash past the mouth of their cave. After a while they heard a rumbling in the sky where the fireball would go down later. There came the whisper of the rain beginning to descend into the leaves of the trees and making its way through them to the ground. The children were returning.

"We'll get wet, Anna," said the boy.

"Who cares?"

"Here's a cave."

"Let's go in, Carl," said Anna, and she scrambled under the cave's roof and inside where the light was dim. "Phew," she said, and then, "oh!"

Anna could scarcely see the pair of birds that cowered against the farthest wall and hissed at her.

Carl followed his sister in. "What is it?"

"Look."

The baby birds raised their wings, defiant. They were afraid! Where was their mother? One of them threw his lunch up on the floor.

"Ugh," Carl said.

"They're buzzards," said Anna.

"No. Buzzards are black and big and redheaded." Carl made a face.

"These are babies, and I'm going to take one home. Their mother won't mind because she'll have the other to take care of."

"Papa won't let you keep it. Ask him for a lamb like mine, Anna," Carl urged.

"I'll tell Papa I'll feed the hens for him every day, and he'll let me keep it."

"Who knows?" she said. "But let *me* do the talking for a change, Carl."

She petted the puppies, and they barked, and the baby bird hissed at them from her arm. "Down," Anna told the dogs, and they ran behind her as she went up to Papa.

He said the same thing that Carl had. "Ugh, Anna. Nobody anywhere ever likes buzzards." And he shook his head. "Buzzards are beautiful only when they're flying. On the ground they're no good. Take it back to its nest now."

"Anna's going to feed the chickens for you, Papa," Carl said. "If she may keep it."

"Didn't I say to be quiet, Carl?" Anna told him. And she said to Papa, "Not only that, but I'll gather the eggs noon and night. I'll hunt for the nests the hens hide out in the yard and under the barn. Let me keep it, Papa."

Papa thought for a moment, and then he looked into his daughter's eyes that were like blue flowers and hopeful. "It's a bargain, Anna. We'll see if you can keep it up all summer long. But I must say, I don't know why anyone would want a buzzard for a pet."

"I'd like a change from puppies," Anna explained. She looked down at the odorous, fluffy, dirt-covered bird.

Anna could scarcely see the pair of birds that cowered against the farthest wall and hissed at her.

Carl followed his sister in. "What is it?"

"Look."

The baby birds raised their wings, defiant. They were afraid! Where was their mother? One of them threw his lunch up on the floor.

"Ugh," Carl said.

"They're buzzards," said Anna.

"No. Buzzards are black and big and redheaded." Carl made a face.

"These are babies, and I'm going to take one home. Their mother won't mind because she'll have the other to take care of."

"Papa won't let you keep it. Ask him for a lamb like mine, Anna," Carl urged.

"I'll tell Papa I'll feed the hens for him every day, and he'll let me keep it."

"No, he won't." The boy shook his head. "Because nobody anywhere ever likes a buzzard."

"I'll gather all the eggs for Papa." And Anna picked up one of the hissing birds and tucked it under her arm.

Carl was used to his stubborn sister who was two years older than he, and eight. "Then let's go, Anna, for I can't stand the smell in here any longer."

The children crawled with the buzzard out into the daylight and the rain of the young summer. They took long barefoot steps upon the damp moss and over the slippery rocks, heading down the hillside to the farm in the valley. The baby buzzard wriggled and then lay still in Anna's arms. It thought perhaps this happened to all baby buzzards.

Papa saw them coming from the loft of the barn and waved his pitchfork. He was in the haymow door where a great swing hung from two thick ropes. The children could sit in it and push their feet and swing out. They looked down upon their whole world. The valley went off one way, and up on the hill they saw the woods, where above the trees sometimes, a black eaglelike bird would float and wheel and then come down for a while.

"What have you got there, Anna!" Papa shouted. "Another puppy from the neighbors? Why don't you raise a nice well-behaved lamb instead!"

Papa was used to Anna and her pets. He laughed and tossed his fork upon the hay he'd thrown below in the barnyard. Then he climbed down the outside ladder in the still falling rain to give the hay to the calves and to Carl's lamb watching and bleating from a nearby pen. Papa never minded rain himself, and he told Mama what she didn't believe, that rain was good for children and made them, and not only crops, grow fast.

"Will Papa know it's a buzzard, Anna?" Carl whispered, as they ducked through the bars of the wood barnyard gate, where Anna's three puppies were waiting and wagging their tails.

"Who knows?" she said. "But let *me* do the talking for a change, Carl."

She petted the puppies, and they barked, and the baby bird hissed at them from her arm. "Down," Anna told the dogs, and they ran behind her as she went up to Papa.

He said the same thing that Carl had. "Ugh, Anna. Nobody anywhere ever likes buzzards." And he shook his head. "Buzzards are beautiful only when they're flying. On the ground they're no good. Take it back to its nest now."

"Anna's going to feed the chickens for you, Papa," Carl said. "If she may keep it."

"Didn't I say to be quiet, Carl?" Anna told him. And she said to Papa, "Not only that, but I'll gather the eggs noon and night. I'll hunt for the nests the hens hide out in the yard and under the barn. Let me keep it, Papa."

Papa thought for a moment, and then he looked into his daughter's eyes that were like blue flowers and hopeful. "It's a bargain, Anna. We'll see if you can keep it up all summer long. But I must say, I don't know why anyone would want a buzzard for a pet."

"I'd like a change from puppies," Anna explained. She looked down at the odorous, fluffy, dirt-covered bird.

"It will fly away in late fall," Papa warned her, "when its black feathers are in and all the other turkey vultures go south for the winter."

Anna wasn't listening. She frowned. "Whatever will Mama say!"

Papa laughed and pulled one of his daughter's yellow braids. "Do you think she'll say to give it a bath first thing? Now run along, all of you." Papa whistled as he pitched the hay to the calves and the lamb.

Mama said just about what Papa predicted she would. She sighed and turned from the kitchen sink. She put her hands on her hips and looked down at the two barefoot ones, who'd made mud tracks all across her fresh-scrubbed floor. "I don't know why your papa says you can go out in the rain. And if he's letting you keep that bird, it'll have to have a bath first thing!"

"Do you mind it, Mama?" Anna hugged the baby buzzard, quiet now, against her dress.

Mama wrinkled her nose. "Wouldn't you rather have a lamb, like Carl's?"

"Everyone says that! And I've been thinking that if you'll let me raise the bird, Mama, I ought to do something in return. I'll wash the breakfast dishes every day, if you like."

"Anna's stubborn," Carl said. "She's promised Papa something, too."

"Don't talk so much, Carl," Anna sighed.

Mama declared, "Promises are made to be kept. We'll see if Anna can keep hers!" And she went to the pantry and brought back two little tubs and a box of soap flakes and some worn-out towels. She put them on the porch.

"Thank you, Mama!" Anna said, her blue eyes bright.

The rain was quitting. Mama and Carl went to heat some milk for the bottle for Carl's baby lamb.

Anna left the buzzard near the doorstep while she went to the water trough to fill one tub with soapsuds and the other with clear rinse water.

The puppies made a circle around the baby bird and sniffed at it, whining. It ducked its head and breathed out a lengthy, low hiss. It was worried, turning about on its big-clawed feet and hoping the three little dogs would stay at bay. Overhead, in the slowly bluing sky, there came out of the mists the flaming ball that the young buzzard had glimpsed every evening under the roof rim of the dusky cave. It wished it were back there and put its head down so its beak almost touched the ground. It kept one eye on the ring of dogs.

Anna came to pick it up. She carried it to the suds and dunked the baby bird in. She patted the soaked feathers so they would be cleaned of the dirt from the cave floor and the smell of the remains of the food its mother had brought it since it hatched from the egg a month ago. Anna was careful to keep the soap out of its eyes and washed the top of the downy head with one finger.

The frightened hiss was subsiding; the buzzard wasn't sure that all its fellows weren't washed in the same way, each by a small blue-eyed pigtailed girl. Anna lifted it from the soapy tub to put it in the rinse water and swish it up and down. Then she dried it with the towels and wrapped it in the one with the least holes. She took it to the house and sat in a chair to rub it a while.

Mama looked at the bedraggled pair and clucked. "I ought to be used to you, Anna, but I'm not! Whatever do you see in that bird?"

"Do you think you'll like it better when it's older, Mama," Anna asked, "and you're used to it?"

"I doubt that." Mama shook her head.

"I even think it's beautiful," Anna said.

"But it isn't," Mama said.

"Look at its yellow-green eyes!" Anna was hopeful.

"I'm glad it's clean, anyway," Mama told her. "And you may keep it in the kitchen until it's dry, Anna."

"Thank you, Mama."

Anna set the baby buzzard in the corner by the stove. She ran out to pick up the tubs and the towels and put them away where they belonged. Then she started doing some of the many things she had promised. She scattered corn in the hen yard and called, "Come, chick, chick, chick!" They dashed to her from all directions. She filled the feed pans with mash and the buckets with water. She got the baskets from the porch and began to hunt and gather eggs.

When she returned finally to the house, there was a change in the buzzard. Because of its bath, all the baby feathers were puffed out and snow-white.

"Look, Mama!"

But Mama was too busy—hurrying back and forth, getting supper. She had poured the cake batter into the tins and shoved them into the oven; the sweet smell was filling the kitchen. Mama stirred the pan bubbling before her on the stove. She took down a skillet and waved it at Anna and the bird.

"Out of the house with you two!"

The buzzard was watching Anna with a quiet eye. Anna picked it up and left the room.

That night, when she fed her three puppies, Anna fixed an extra portion of the same food and brought it out to set before the baby buzzard. It nibbled and turned the food about in the dish. But it could not eat. It felt a yearning for the half-dark cave and its fellow there, and for the great rushing sound of their mother's wings as she came down through the trees, bringing their supper. Anna went to fill a cup with water and put it beside the bird. After a while it dipped its beak in and put its head back to let the water run down its throat.

Carl came nearby to watch. "What's its name, Anna? Everything has to have a name."

"I can't make up my mind, Carl! Don't ask me yet."

But Anna did make it up that night when she took the bird out to the lamb's stall to sleep. It hissed at the unfamiliar scent of the barn and at the maaing of the lamb. Anna put it on the edge of the manger, and it perched there unsteadily.

She heard Mama calling that it was bedtime and tomorrow was another day and Anna must come in at once. Anna gave the bird a noble name then and told it to Papa when she said goodnight.

"Glory is lonesome, Papa."

"Why don't you call it Joe?" Papa asked. "Or Jane or Mary?"

"How do I know if it's a boy or a girl? Its name is Glory."

"That's the most *un*glorious bird I ever saw!" Papa laughed.

"I'm calling it that in hope, Papa!"

"It looks that way." And Papa looked into Anna's blue eyes. "Did you ever make a wish on a buzzard, Anna?"

"How do you do that, Papa?"

"If you see one flying and wish on it, and then it dips its wing before it's out of sight, your wish will come true."

As Anna went to sleep, she thought how she knew what she'd wish right now: that her bird felt at home and not lonely any longer.

In the morning Anna had trouble sitting still while Mama braided her hair at breakfast. "Supposing Carl's lamb has stepped on Glory, Mama!"

"Glory would get out of the way," Carl said, scornful, from where he ate his cereal across from Anna.

At last breakfast was over, and Anna fed her puppies quickly. She told Mama, "I'll be back to wash the dishes. Remember I'm doing them!" And she ran to the barn with a bowl of food for the baby buzzard. She found it had hopped down from the manger and lay stretched out in the straw not far from the sleepy lamb. It got up and came to gobble the breakfast this time, while Anna watched.

Then when Anna was feeding the chickens and gathering the eggs, she kept her bird nearby. Glory began to follow Anna about. She went into the house to wash the dishes and left Glory on the porch in the sunlight. When she was finished, and came out of the door, the bird was standing with wings outstretched in the way of buzzards. Its shadow stood before on the wooden porch floor, in the shape of a T. It turned a little this way and that, wanting the sun to strike every downy white feather.

Anna was delighted. "Glory, you look like a baby angel!"

The summer that began then for Anna was nicer than any had ever been before. Time went by in the slow soft way that summer has. Bees droned about the red clover blooms, and butterflies fluttered in the daisies where Papa's cows and sheep grazed. The three puppies began to look more like dogs. Carl's lamb got fat and thick-wooled, and his voice changed from a high to a low baa. One morning he refused his bottle when Carl offered it to him.

"Everything changes," Papa told the children. "Look at Glory."

For now the young buzzard's white down was mingled with black feathers. And when Anna put Glory on the edge of the old wagon down in the field, while she lay on her stomach underneath to read a book, the bird's wings spread out five feet in the sun.

Sometimes Anna went up in the barn loft to sit in the swing. Glory would crouch in the hay and watch her. The buzzard would cock its head on one side, a yellow-green eye on the girl flying back and forth—out over the barnyard into the brilliant light and back into the shadowy mow where the hay was piled.

"One day *you*'ll fly!" Anna told the bird. "I have to hold onto the ropes, but you'll be able to let go, Glory."

On a hot afternoon, Anna and Carl went up into the woods. The dogs followed, and Carl's lamb, and Glory too, tagging after Anna's bare feet. The bird ducked its head, affectionate, every time Anna turned to see if it were still coming. It liked to play and would pick up sticks she threw and carry them about as it followed Anna.

As they approached the cave where the children had first found Glory, there was a great flapping of wings and the black mother vulture flew up through the trees. The dogs growled, but the young bird never even noticed. Its eyes were on Anna, whom it thought of as its parent.

They reached the cave and heard the alarmed soft hiss inside. But Glory paid no heed to the sound of its cave-mate

either, staying close to the girl whom it thought of as its own
kind now. Since Anna fed Glory only the puppies' food and
table scraps, the tame buzzard didn't even have the odor of
the wild baby. It had no more scent than Carl's lamb or
Anna's young dogs had.

Anna laughed, running on bare feet through the trees,
over the mossy ground, back down toward the farm again.
The sun gleamed on the green hillside. The three dogs

yelped about which of them ran the fastest. Glory held both wings out for balance and skipped and hopped after Anna. The lamb leaped sidewise into the air and dashed ahead of Carl, who shouted:

"Wait for me, everybody!"

Anna called back at her brother into the heated, yellow air, "I hope this summer lasts forever and ever, Carl!" It seemed to Anna that it might.

Toward the last of August, even Mama began to like Glory. While Anna had been in the barnyard looking for eggs, the three dogs had slipped into the kitchen. They had stolen a roast of beef from a pot in the middle of the table. It was the family's supper, and Mama called Papa. He fastened a hook on the kitchen door.

"Now they won't do it again, Mama," he said, swinging his hammer.

Anna came up with a basket of eggs in each hand, and Mama told her, "One thing I'll say for your baby buzzard: it wouldn't have done that. It's got manners!" Mama looked fierce.

"That's right," Papa said. "And now what are we going to eat?"

"I'll fry some of those eggs Anna's brought." Mama took the baskets from Anna. "But I wouldn't mind if it were Anna's dogs that flew down south this fall—and her bird that stayed!" And Mama marched back into the kitchen.

"Is Glory going to fly away?" Carl turned to Anna.

"That's the silliest thing I ever heard!" she cried.

"I'm glad I've got a lamb who can't go anywhere," Carl said.

"I'd rather have Glory just the same." And Anna bent to pick up the bird at her feet. She was frowning because she'd forgotten all about Papa's saying that Glory would fly south when the other turkey vultures did for the winter.

School began suddenly. Mama said to Anna at the table, "You don't need to do the breakfast dishes anymore."

Anna said, "I'll still do them on weekends, because I like to help, Mama."

"Thank you, Anna," Mama said.

Papa told Anna, "Now that you're back in school, I'll gather the eggs and feed the hens, too."

"I'll still take care of the hens on weekends," Anna said, "because I want to help you, Papa."

"Thank you, Anna," said Papa. "I've never been able to find as many hidden nests as you."

Mama had gotten out two tin lunch buckets from the pantry. In each she put a bunch of Concord grapes, a hard-boiled egg, peanut butter and jam sandwiches that she wrapped in brown paper, and a thermos of milk. Carl waved back at his lamb, who stood with the dogs at the farm gate. The lamb put his feet up on the bars and baaed after Carl. Anna had to lock Glory in the barn so the bird wouldn't follow; Papa promised to let Glory out later.

When Anna came home that night, the buzzard was no-where to be found. Finally Anna spotted Glory in one of the trees, on a low branch. It was the first time the bird had got off the ground. Anna went for a saucer of food for it, and Glory spread broad wings and glided down to eat. Anna saw then what she had not really noticed before—that every white baby feather had been replaced by a black shiny one. Glory was beautiful and eaglelike!

When the bird had finished the food, it flapped its wings. Anna saw that they were six feet across. Glory ran about the yard, skipping, picking up sticks and carrying them about, one eye on the girl, delighted at her return.

Anna told her, "Glory! You came up to all my hopes when I named you that."

Papa called to them from the barn door where he stood with pails in his hands, about to milk the cows. "Next year this time, Glory will have a red head, Anna!"

"I'm not thinking about Glory's looks, Papa," she shouted back, "but about flying away!"

"I never heard before of anyone anywhere liking a buz-zard or having one around," Papa cried. "So I can't say for sure what yours will do. Go or stay." And Papa went in.

"Do as you please, Glory," Anna told her bird, firm.

Every afternoon when Anna returned, she would find the buzzard off in some tree. She would call, "Here, Glory!" And the bird would come down and want to play and follow her to the kitchen porch, where Anna gave it food. At night it still roosted on the manger of the stall where the lamb was asleep.

The autumn winds were beginning to blow outside the house and barn. Some of the trees were speckled and spotted with yellow and red, and some were all clothed in a bright color. Later the leaves would fall in piles and be whirled and scattered. One suppertime, Papa said: "Today I read in the paper, Anna, that the turkey vultures have been seen flying south. I thought you would want to know."

Anna nodded. "I do. Thank you for telling me, Papa." Her blue eyes were quiet.

"And they say," he told Anna, "that most buzzards return in spring to whatever place they came from."

Mama said, "Don't feel badly, Anna. Glory will come back. You know I like that bird, and I never thought I would at first."

"I like Glory too, Anna," said Papa.

"So do I," said Carl. "And we thought that nobody anywhere ever liked buzzards!"

"Just hearing that most of them come back in spring makes me feel better," Anna told them.

"Anna's growing up," said Mama. She patted Anna's cheek.

"She kept her summer bargains, too, and we didn't know if she would," said Papa. He pulled Anna's braids, and smiled into her eyes, so she laughed in spite of her worry.

The next day Anna couldn't find her bird when she came home from school. Her three young dogs went with her while she hunted all over the farm. Finally she gave up. Carl's lamb had no company that night in his stall.

A week later, when Anna and the dogs were out again, she spied the black speck in the sky. It came closer, wheeling and floating. When the bird was almost overhead, it folded its wings and came down into a tree.

Anna called, "Glory, here!"

And it glided from the branch to her feet. It ducked its head and put its bill to the ground and looked sidewise at Anna. She put out her arm and the buzzard climbed onto the sleeve of her coat and rode on it while she walked to the porch. She set it on the railing. The dogs were used to the

bird and paid no heed. They went to lie near the door and flop their tails whenever Anna passed by them.

After Glory had eaten, the bird preened its feathers a while in the cold breeze. Anna sat on the step and watched. She could feel the restless urge in the creature, which would make its journey now out of instinct. It would join other turkey vultures who came together, young and old, in a warm land to wait out the winter season before they came back to nest and raise their young in the north. The same impulse that guided the bird from her would bring Glory back. Anna knew it was trying to say goodbye now, and that it wouldn't even stay one more night in the barn.

The sun was almost falling under the earth's rim. Papa was leading and driving all the farm animals into the warm barn. Carl was helping. Anna could hear their calls and laughter.

Glory opened wide wings and flapped them slowly. The buzzard turned to look at Anna, its yellow-green eyes bright. Then it was taking to the air in an easy and sure fashion, higher and higher. Anna watched it soar, and knew that somehow, vaguely, the young buzzard thought of itself as a small girl with braids and blue eyes and bare feet that flew

once in a while back and forth in a swing in a haymow doorway.

"Go or come as you please, Glory," Anna whispered. "It's up to you."

Then, as the bird grew smaller and smaller, flying toward the ball of fire in the west, Anna saw it dip its wing. She could hear Mama in the kitchen and Papa and Carl calling to each other in the barn. Mama came onto the porch to announce about dinner being ready and that tomorrow would come before they knew it and everybody must come in at once.

Anna petted the three dogs as she turned to go in. And she was making a wish.